Snowbound!

Behind a small clump of trees, Sasha saw a little hut.

"I'll go in there," muttered Sasha. "Maybe I can keep warm till Father comes to look for me."

When he reached it he pushed the door open. It was bare and deserted.

"At least it will protect me from the snow," Sasha said to himself. As his eyes got used to the dark, he saw that there was a pile of logs in one corner. Then he realized that the hut wasn't deserted, and that he wasn't alone.

In a corner sat a little wolf with shining eyes and sharp teeth.

OTHER PUFFIN CHAPTERS YOU MAY ENJOY

SASHA
AND THE
WOLFCUB

Ann Jungman
Illustrated by Cliff Wright

PUFFIN BOOKS

PUFFIN BOOKS
Published by the Penguin Group
Penguin Putnam Inc., 375 Hudson Street, New York, New York 10014, U.S.A.
Penguin Books Ltd, 27 Wrights Lane, London W8 5TZ, England
Penguin Books Australia Ltd, Ringwood, Victoria, Australia
Penguin Books Canada Ltd, 10 Alcorn Avenue, Toronto, Ontario, Canada M4V 3B2
Penguin Books (N.Z.) Ltd, 182-190 Wairau Road, Auckland 10, New Zealand

Penguin Books Ltd, Registered Offices: Harmondsworth, Middlesex, England

First published in Great Britain by CollinsChildren's Books, 1996
Published in Puffin Books, 1998

1 3 5 7 9 10 8 6 4 2

LIBRARY OF CONGRESS CATALOGING-IN-PUBLICATION DATA
Jungman, Ann.
Sasha and the wolfcub / Ann Jungman ; illustrated by Cliff Wright.
p. cm.
Summary: One snowy winter in long-ago Russia, a young boy and a talking
wolf cub meet when they both get lost and after some years, they find a way
to end the animosity between the villagers and the wolves.
ISBN 0-14-038833-8 (pbk.)
[1. Wolves—Fiction. 2. Russia—Fiction.] I. Wright, Cliff, ill. II. Title.
PZ7.J957Sas 1998 [Fic]—dc21 97-28174 CIP AC

Printed in the United States of America

RL: 2.9

To Graham and Jennifer, with love

CHAPTER 1

*I*t was winter in the village. This year, as every year, when the days shortened, snow began to fall until a thick blanket covered everything. Sasha stood on the porch of his wooden house and looked out at the vast white steppe, silent and mysterious. Sasha didn't mind the snow because he had thick boots, a fur cap, and many layers of clothing to keep him warm. Like most children, Sasha liked it best when a blanket of snow covered the world, when all the rooftops had a thick layer of crisp whiteness and the trees had a canopy of silver snow that seemed to glisten magically pink in the setting sun.

"Now we'll be able to have snow fights," Sasha said to his mother, grinning broadly, "and go skating on the village pond, and maybe this winter Father will let me drive the sleigh on my own."

Then out from the vast white steppe came an eerie noise, the sound of howling.

"There are the wolves," said Sasha's mother. "That shows winter is really here. They are hungry and are coming near to the village to steal our food and animals. Now you just be careful, Sasha, hungry wolves are dangerous."

Just then another sound came ringing

through the crisp winter air, the jolly sound of sleigh bells. Into the village swept Sasha's father, Ivan, in his big sleigh drawn by two horses.

"Hello there, Sasha. Just listen to the wolves howling. What a cold night, aye?"

"It is cold, Father," replied Sasha. "Wonderfully cold!"

"Wonderfully cold," laughed Ivan. "What nonsense you talk." He got out of the sleigh and gave his son a rough hug.

"Father, please can I drive the sleigh on my own? Just once."

"It's too dangerous, my boy, now that the wolves are howling."

"Oh please, Father, just one ride – please, you promised."

Ivan relented. "All right; but once round the village and straight back here, mind."

Sasha leapt into the sleigh, grabbed the reins of the horses and off he went. He drove through the village, past the

frozen pond, past the church, past the great house, and then he was out alone on the vast open steppe. Sasha felt the wind on his face and the reins in his hands and saw the horses racing happily in front of him. He forgot all about his father's warnings and his promise to drive only once round the village. He drove on and on and on, farther and farther into the white wilderness.

Suddenly the sleigh hit something hard and Sasha was thrown out. He landed head first in the snow. After a moment he managed to sit up and look around but the horses and sleigh had gone and he was alone in the middle of the steppe. There was nothing to be seen but white snow all around him. The sun was almost out of sight; soon it would be dark and it was beginning to snow again. If only he had listened to his father! Sasha felt very scared. Then, behind a small clump of trees, he saw a little hut.

"I'll go in there," muttered Sasha. "Maybe I can keep warm till Father comes to look for me."

So Sasha struggled towards the hut.

When he reached it he pushed the door open. It was bare and deserted; a simple hut made from wood, used by woodmen in the summer.

"At least it will protect me from the snow," Sasha said to himself, and he rubbed his hands together and stamped his feet. As his eyes got used to the dark, he saw that there was a pile of logs in one corner. Then he realised that the hut wasn't deserted, and that he wasn't alone.

In a corner sat a little wolf with shining eyes and sharp teeth.

CHAPTER 2

Sasha looked at the wolf and the wolf looked at Sasha. There was silence. Then, to Sasha's amazement, the wolf said fiercely, "If you're coming in, come in and shut the door and if you're going out, go out and shut the door, but don't just stand there letting the snow in."

"Sorry," said Sasha, quickly shutting the door. "Is this your hut?"

"Finders keepers," replied the wolf rudely. "But I don't live here, if that's what you mean. I'm lost."

"I suppose you're one of the wolves who was howling outside my village?"

"'Spect so," answered the wolf, "or was till I got lost."

"You're not very big for a wolf," commented Sasha.

"And you're not very big for a man," snapped the wolf.

"But I'm not a man," explained Sasha, "I'm a child."

"Well, I'm not a wolf, I'm a cub, and you can be glad that I'm not a fully-grown wolf or you'd be in big trouble."

"That's not nice," protested Sasha.

"Well, if you had a gun I bet you'd have taken a shot at me. People are scared of wolves. You wouldn't be talking to me now, I bet," said the wolf.

"I suppose not," Sasha agreed sadly.

The wolfcub began to walk up and down and bang his paws together.

"Are you cold?" asked Sasha, who was shivering himself.

"No, man-child. Wolves don't get cold," said the wolfcub, trying not to show that he was shivering. "Wolves are tough. Still, if you had some matches, I would go out on the wide white steppe and find some kindling and we could make a fire from those logs. Not that I'm cold, mind you, just that it's more friendly."

"I've got some matches," said Sasha, cheering up. "If you go and get the kindling, I'll look and see if I can find some food."

A little later Sasha and the wolfcub were sitting beside a blazing fire.

"I've found some frozen goat in the corner," said Sasha. "We could cook it and eat it."

"Don't you dare cook my bit!" snapped the wolfcub. "I eat mine red and raw."

Sasha handed the wolfcub a chunk of

meat and he gnawed at it eagerly and waited for it to soften. Sasha watched his bit sizzle and spit as it cooked in the fire.

"My name is Ferdy," the wolfcub said amiably. "Do men-children have names?"

"Of course we do," replied Sasha. "Mine's Sasha."

"What are you doing out here all on your own, anyway?" asked Ferdy.

"I went for a ride alone in my father's sleigh and I got thrown out. Father told me not to go too far but I got carried away."

"So I see," sighed Ferdy. "I went exploring on my own, too. 'You stick with the pack, Ferdy,' my parents said, 'and you'll be all right.' But I had to go off and see the world for myself, and I end up by a fire with a man-child called Sasha."

Sasha noticed blood on one of Ferdy's paws. "Hey, Ferdy, you've hurt your paw."

"It's nothing," snapped Ferdy. "A tiny scratch. Wolves don't make a fuss about things like that. Wolves are tough," and he gave his paw a lick but the scratch still bled.

"Maybe I should put a little bandage on it to stop the bleeding," said Sasha.

"Wolves don't have bandages."

"Not even a very little bandage? Look, I'll tear a strip off my best shirt that my Auntie Masha embroidered for me."

"Well, just to please you," Ferdy agreed reluctantly.

So Sasha tore a strip off his beautiful shirt and tied up Ferdy's foot.

"It does help," confessed the wolfcub as Sasha tied the knot.

"Good, now we can be friends for ever," said Sasha, smiling.

"Don't be silly," snapped the wolf.

"Why is it silly?" demanded Sasha.

"It just is," grumbled the wolfcub. "Everyone knows that."

"You still haven't given me a reason," Sasha pointed out.

"People and wolves have always been enemies," snapped Ferdy. "I know, because my mum told me and my dad told me and all my uncles and aunts and all the wolves in the pack told me, so it must be true."

"I've always been told that wolves were all bad," said Sasha hotly, "but that doesn't make it true."

"Look, in a couple of years we won't even recognize each other," explained Ferdy. "I'll be just like any other wolf and you'll be just like all the men with guns. So even if we wanted to be friends we couldn't."

"Maybe you're right," sighed Sasha. "But it does seem a shame, we're getting on so well sitting beside this fire. You eat your meat raw and I eat mine cooked but that doesn't mean we can't be friends. Why can't people and wolves get on?"

"Oh dear," groaned Ferdy. "Sasha, man-child, you don't understand! Here it is just me, Ferdy, and you, Sasha, but usually wolves and men don't even get a chance to talk. It's only because we are both lost and little that we've even got this far. When we get back to our homes, we'll think and behave just like all the others."

"I know, but isn't it a pity?" replied Sasha.

"Oh, I don't know," mused Ferdy, "I expect I'll quite like being a big bad wolf."

"If we shared our food with you," Sasha asked Ferdy, "would you stop stealing and killing?"

"'Course we would," sniffed Ferdy. "What a daft question, 'course we would. Food's what it's all about."

After they'd finished eating, they told each other stories about their lives. Gradually the warmth of the fire and all the eating and talking made them tired. Sasha yawned and then Ferdy yawned and stretched.

"I'm going to take a little nap," announced Ferdy. "Wake me if anything happens," and he fell asleep.

Sasha tried hard to keep awake but, after putting a few extra logs on the fire, he curled up round Ferdy and fell asleep too.

CHAPTER 3

Sasha woke suddenly; he could hear the tinkling of bells. It took him a moment or two to realize where he was.

"It must be Father coming for me," he thought, and then he shook Ferdy. "Hey, Ferdy, wake up, I can hear bells. It's probably my father in a sleigh, searching for me. He'll have seen the smoke."

The wolfcub sat up quickly and listened. "The pack aren't far away either, man-child, I can hear them howling. I expect my dad has come looking for me too."

Sasha ran and looked out of the door. "My father is not far off now. You've got to hide, Ferdy: he'll have a gun. Father doesn't like wolves. Hide here, under this sack."

"Right," said Ferdy. "Good thinking, man-child." He grabbed the sack and hid behind the pile of wood. "Psst, Sasha," whispered Ferdy, sticking his nose out from behind the wood, "get your dad out of here quickly. The pack are very near."

"Thanks, Ferdy. Bye," Sasha whispered back as he walked towards the door of the hut.

"Sasha, Sasha," came a voice from the darkness outside. "Sasha, are you there?"

"Here I am, Father," cried Sasha, flinging the door open. "Oh, I am so glad to see you."

Ivan gathered Sasha in a big hug. "You're safe, my boy, you're safe," he cried. "We've been so worried. How could you do such a crazy thing? Wait here, I'll get some furs from the sleigh, and then it's home for you as fast as possible."

"Goodbye, Ferdy," Sasha whispered as his father went for the furs. "Good luck!"

"Goodbye, man-child. Have a good life!"

As Sasha travelled back to the village Ivan scolded him. "We've been so worried about you. Your mother is desperate. Sasha, you should know better; the wolves could have got you. Just listen to the beasts, they are howling louder than ever."

Sasha listened. He thought he could hear Ferdy's voice howling with the rest of the pack – he even thought he saw a little white paw waving to him as he sped home to the hot soup his mother had ready for him.

* * *

A few days later Sasha was walking home from school when he heard a familiar voice.

"Psst-psst. Over here, man-child." Sasha looked up and saw a white paw beckoning to him. Sasha hurried over, smiling broadly.

"Hello, Ferdy! How nice to see you again."

"You take this silly bandage off," snapped Ferdy. "Take it off right now!"

"Is your paw really better then?"

"Don't worry about that. This bandage is making me a laughing stock. Now take it off or I'll bite your ears."

"All right," said Sasha. "But you don't have to be so rude."

"The other wolves said I'd gone soft.

It's all your fault, so you just watch it, man-child."

"You wouldn't harm me, Ferdy."

"Honestly, Sasha man-child, you worry me. You have a mother and a father and you go to school, but you don't seem to know a thing about life. What do they teach you at school about wolves?"

"They tell us that wolves are

dangerous," said Sasha. "When the wolves come too near the village, shooting parties go out. A wolf was killed last week."

"I know," muttered Ferdy. "It was my brother," and he ran round in circles, burying his head in the snow every now and then.

"Oh, poor Ferdy," Sasha said sympathetically.

"Don't be sorry for me. Wolves are very tough and don't you forget it."

"Then why are you running round in circles like that?"

"It's just something wolves do," snapped Ferdy. "And I have lots of other brothers. We wolves live in packs and we're just like one big family; we all look after each other and we share everything and all the big wolves look after all the little wolves, so there. And if you make another comment I'll eat your toes." With that, Ferdy ran off into the wood, laughing.

Sasha wondered if he would ever see Ferdy again but as the months went by he forgot all about the wolf.

CHAPTER 4

One day, when spring was just around the corner and the snow was starting to melt, the village held a dance. The village square was decorated with branches and blossoms and there were tables loaded with delicious food, and over a big open fire an ox was being roasted. Everyone wore their best clothes. The band played happily and people danced. Sasha stood on the porch, tapping his feet, while his parents joined in the celebrations.

Round and round they went, heels clicking, skirts swirling, the men clapping and shouting. After a while the men began to leap up in the air and click their heels together. Higher and higher they went and Sasha watched and laughed as he clapped to encourage his father and the other men.

Then, above all the noise, Sasha heard a voice that sounded familiar. "Psst-psst, Sasha man-child. Psst! Over here."

Sasha looked round. There was no one to be seen so he walked round to the back of the house, and there sat Ferdy watching the spectacle.

"Hey, Sasha, what's going on? Have they all gone mad?"

"No, Ferdy, it's dancing, it's what

people do when they are happy."

"Would you show me how to dance?"

"Of course I will, Ferdy, but not now."

The wolf looked very disappointed. "But I want to dance now, this very minute. That music makes me want to jump in the air and leap about."

"But, Ferdy, you might get caught."

"Don't worry, they're all too busy enjoying themselves to think about wolves. Come on, let's get started. No time like the present."

"Oh, all right," said Sasha. "You go and stand over there and then you skip towards me and then hold my hand."

"That sounds easy," said Ferdy, happily. "One, two, three, go!" And he bounced towards Sasha on all fours.

"No, Ferdy, you can't dance like that. You have to stand up."

"Just because people do," complained Ferdy, but he stood on his hind legs, draped his tail over one arm, put his nose in the air, and skipped elegantly towards Sasha. Soon the two were dancing very well.

"I like dancing," said Ferdy. "It is one good thing people do." Then he put his head round the corner of the house. "Just look at that," he breathed.

"Oh, that's just some of the men doing a Cossack dance," explained Sasha, as the men leapt in the air with crossed arms, kicking their legs out in front and shouting.

"I'll show you." Sasha folded his arms,

crouched down and kicked his legs out into the air until he fell over backwards.

"I'm going to try," said Ferdy, and he folded his front paws and began to kick, but he fell over straightaway. "I can't do it."

"That's because you need boots to do Cossack dancing."

"Boots, aye?" said Ferdy. "I see. Well, goodbye, Sasha man-child. I must go back to the pack now," and off he sped as silently as he had come.

Later that night Sasha woke up feeling cold. He sat up in bed and noticed that his shutters were open and that there was an odd noise outside. He got out of bed and peeped out of the window. There was Ferdy, wearing Sasha's boots, practising Cossack dancing.

"Ferdy, Ferdy," hissed Sasha. "You come here at once and give me back my boots."

Ferdy grinned his wicked wolf's grin, waved and went on dancing.

"Ferdy, stop it," whispered Sasha. "If you wake anyone else up you'll be in real trouble."

"Good point," said Ferdy and climbed into Sasha's bedroom. "I like that dancing. Can I keep the boots?"

"Of course you can't. How could I manage without my boots? I couldn't go to school or anything. Come on, Ferdy, you know it's too cold for me to go out without my boots. I couldn't go anywhere in the winter. My feet would freeze."

"Sasha," came his mother's voice. "Are your shutters open?"

"Er yes – the wind must have done it. I'll close them straightaway," called Sasha, as Ferdy slipped under the bed and lay flat on his back.

"Really, Sasha," said his mother as she came into the room, "you must be more careful, the wolves could get in."

"Stop worrying, Mother," mumbled Sasha in a sleepy voice. Then he yawned and said, "I'm tired, I'm going back to sleep. Good night, Mother."

"Good night, little one," said his mother, leaning over to kiss him. Her foot touched Ferdy but she left the room without noticing him.

Ferdy put his head out. "Has she gone? Whew! That was a narrow escape," commented the wolf as he wriggled out from under the bed.

"Ferdy, you must go."

"Please, please, let me take the boots," begged the wolf. "I stuffed the boots full of socks so that they would fit me. I'll give you back all the socks, if I can just have the boots."

"No, not my boots. You can have anything else you want."

"I only want the boots. In the hut you said, 'I'm your friend, Ferdy. What's mine is yours.' Well some friend you are. That's people for you. So, if it's no boots, it's no friendship." And Ferdy jumped out of the window, leaving Sasha feeling guilty.

"Oh, well," Sasha comforted himself, "Ferdy didn't really need the boots and I just can't do without them. I expect he'll get over it soon and I'll see him again."

CHAPTER 5

*B*ut Sasha didn't see Ferdy again, not that winter or the next one. He had almost forgotten about the wolf when one snowy day he was walking through a wood with his gun slung over his shoulder. It had been a long and cold winter, and every night the wolves howled loudly outside the village.

"Those brutes are hungry," growled Ivan. "Listen to them out there."

"Poor wolves," said Sasha. "They're

probably cold as well."

"Poor wolves indeed," snapped Ivan. "That any son of mine should talk such rubbish! Now, Sasha, you go that way and I'll go this. We need to clear this area of wolves."

Sasha walked for a while, then he heard a branch creak behind him. He turned, and catching a glimpse of a wolf, aimed his gun straight at the animal. Just as he was about to pull the trigger he lowered the gun and smiled.

"Ferdy!" he cried. "How wonderful to see you."

"What's wonderful about it?" growled the wolf. "I was just going to attack you."

"Well," said Sasha, and grinned. "So you didn't recognize me. I must have

changed more than you."

"I did recognize you, of course I did," muttered the wolf.

"But, Ferdy," said Sasha, "you couldn't attack me any more than I could hurt you."

"I was very hungry," the wolf explained, apologetically. "And I bet you would hurt me if you had to."

"No, I wouldn't," replied Sasha.

"Fine words, man-child," answered Ferdy. "But I don't believe you."

"I'll prove it to you," said Sasha, his eyes blazing. "I'll throw down my gun and walk away from you. Then I will have no protection from you at all," and he flung his gun down onto the snow and marched away. Ferdy looked at him

in amazement but didn't move.

After a minute Sasha turned round. "See, Ferdy, I was right. You couldn't do it. Our friendship means too much to you, too."

"All right," snapped Ferdy. "You win, but don't shout, I don't want the whole pack to know. If you ever tell anyone I'll chew your ears off and bite your nose and ..."

Sasha walked over to Ferdy and gave him a big hug. "Ferdy, this is wonderful."

"Huh," sniffed the wolf.

"It is, it's wonderful, because it means that if people and wolves are friends when they are young, they can be friends later on, too."

"That's all well and good, but I'm still hungry."

"Here, eat my lunch. I'll put food out for you tonight and every night while there's snow on the ground."

"Put out lots," Ferdy told him. "Wolves have to share with the pack, remember."

"I can't leave you much," Sasha told him. "Just what I can save from my dinner – but I'll try to get more."

"Try," sniffed Ferdy. "Try! We can't eat *try*."

"I'm sorry, I'll do what I can, but I'm only one person," Sasha explained, desperately.

Just then Sasha's father called. "Sasha, are you there?"

"Yes, Father, no wolves round here."

Sasha picked up his gun. "Goodbye, Ferdy, it was good to see you again," he said.

"Goodbye, Sasha man-child," replied Ferdy.

That night, when everyone was asleep, Sasha put out what little food he could, and his old pair of boots. The next morning they had gone. Sasha kept his word and left out food every night until the snow melted.

Sasha didn't see Ferdy again for more than two years, but whenever there was a celebration in the village and the band played jolly music and the villagers danced well into the night, Sasha often thought he could see a furry figure on a nearby hill dancing in the moonlight and swirling and leaping higher than any of the men of the village.

CHAPTER 6

One freezing day Ivan announced that he was going to visit the neighbouring village.

"But, Ivan," cried Sasha's mother, "a cold wind is blowing in from the steppe. Today is not a good time to go travelling."

"Mother's right, Father," agreed Sasha. "Please leave it till another day. No business can be *that* important."

"This business can't wait," Ivan replied

grimly. "All the headmen of the local villages are meeting to discuss the wolves."

"The wolves?" said Sasha sharply. "Why the wolves?"

"Because the signs are that this is going to be a particularly long winter. Food will be short and we can't have the wolves taking any of it. We've got to join together to contain the brutes."

"But, Father," argued Sasha, "if we gave some of our food to the wolves they wouldn't steal it and we wouldn't have to be so afraid of them."

"Enough!" shouted his father. "You are no longer a boy, Sasha. Now you are a man you must accept that wolves are our enemies or you will have a short life."

"Why won't you listen to me, Father? Why are you so blind on this matter?"

"I forbid you ever to raise this subject with me again, Sasha. Why did I have to have the only child in all the Russias who does not know that wolves are dangerous, and that hungry wolves are very, very dangerous? Now, out of my way." And Ivan stormed out, leapt into his sleigh and drove off with the bells ringing.

Sasha stood in the doorway, watching his father disappear into the distance, and thought to himself, "I wish I could get word to Ferdy to warn him of what's going on – still, I don't know what good it would do. If only I could get Father to listen. Why can't I think of a way of getting through to him?"

That night Olga, his mother, cooked a huge pot of thick soup.

"Your father will need something hot inside him after that long drive," she told Sasha as she handed him a hot, steaming bowl full of soup, and some bread. Sasha took the bowl and went to sit by the window.

"It's getting dark out there, Mother, he should be back by now," he said.

"The snow is falling very thickly," replied his mother. "I expect that has held him up."

But hour after hour went by, the night got darker and darker, and there was still no sign of Ivan. Sasha and Olga began to get very worried.

"I'm going to borrow the sleigh from Peter and Ludmilla next door," said Sasha. "I'll go and search for Father."

"No, Sasha," cried his mother. "You might get eaten by the wolves."

"You worry too much, Mother," said Sasha, putting his arm round her. "Remember the time when I was thrown from the sleigh on the steppe and you gave me up for lost but Father found me safe and sound?" His mother nodded through her tears. "Well, now the time has come for me to do the same for him."

Olga managed a small smile. "That was the beginning of your talking nonsense about wolves."

"Well, Mother, that's one thing we won't have to worry about with Father." And laughing, Sasha went out to borrow a sleigh.

The steppe was very dark but Sasha managed to follow the stars to find the road to the next village of Noviogorsk. As he drove along he heard the sound of the wolves howling. Sasha listened and thought he heard Ferdy calling, "Over here, Sasha man-child."

"I'm hearing things," thought Sasha. "Maybe I *am* a bit crazy, as Father thinks." Then through the fast-falling snow he saw smoke rising from a hut.

"That's the hut where I met Ferdy," he thought, and he clicked the reins to make the horses go faster. Reaching the hut, Sasha reined in the horses, leapt out of the sleigh and rushed inside. There in the corner was Ivan, slumped on some sacking with his head propped up on a log.

"Father!" cried Sasha. "Thank goodness you're safe!"

Ivan didn't move or reply. Sasha knelt down by his father. Ivan was breathing evenly but there was a big wound on his head.

"He's only unconscious," thought Sasha.

"He'll be all right but I must get him home quickly."

Sasha looked round the hut. The fire was crackling crisply and had plenty of logs on it. "Someone must have rescued Father and brought him here," thought Sasha, then he smiled. "Ferdy, it must have been Ferdy," and he laughed to himself at the joke. "Father saved by a wolf!"

Sasha laid Ivan in the sleigh and covered him with furs, then he set off as fast as he could back to their home. Sasha drove past the great house, past the church, past the frozen pond, and then swept into the village. Everyone was waiting outside their houses.

"It's Sasha and he's got Ivan with him!"

shouted young Evgeny, and a great cheer went up.

Two big men ran forward and carried Ivan into the house and laid him on his bed. Olga bathed his head with cold water while Sasha covered his father with blankets. All the villagers stood round waiting to hear what had happened.

* * *

After a while Ivan sat up and held his head.

"How are you feeling, Father?" asked Sasha.

"Terrible," replied Ivan. "My head feels like it's splitting in two."

"Just lie down and don't try to talk," Olga told him.

Ivan lay down again, groaning. "My head hurts, but what is worse is that I think I'm going crazy. I was driving along, the horses were tired, and then suddenly there was a crashing sound. The horses panicked and overturned the sleigh and I felt a mountain of snow fall on me. I thought I was dead but then – and this is the crazy bit – it seemed as though a wolf pulled me out, dragged me to a hut, put me on some sacking with a log under my head and said, 'It's only because you're Sasha man-child's father,' lit a fire and took off."

The villagers clapped their hands and roared with laughter.

"That's a good one, Ivan," said old Peter, tears running down his face. "A talking wolf!"

"And even if a wolf could talk, it's not likely he'd rescue Ivan the wolf-hater," added Ludmilla, gasping for breath.

"It's the bang on the head," said Olga. "He won't be so fanciful tomorrow."

As the villagers filed out old Peter stopped at the door. He slapped Sasha on the shoulder and doubled up with laughter, saying, "So, young Sasha, it seems a wolf friend of yours saved Ivan's life."

Sasha smiled. "Yes, it does. Indeed it does."

The next day Ivan sat up in bed, his bandaged head propped up by pillows, and held out his arms to Sasha.

"Well, Sasha my boy, it seems I have to thank you for rescuing me."

"No, Father, not me. It's Ferdy you have to thank."

"Ferdy? Who's this Ferdy?"

"My wolf friend, the one who dragged you out of the snow."

"I'm a sick man, Sasha," roared Ivan. "How dare you talk this nonsense to me now!"

"Your father is quite right," agreed Olga angrily. "You shouldn't upset him at such a time."

"But what you told us last night, Father, it's true!"

"Nonsense!" growled Ivan.

"Rubbish!" agreed Olga.

"Well, Father didn't walk out of that avalanche himself, make up a fire, put down a log and some old sacks and then knock himself out," protested Sasha.

His parents were silent for a moment, then Ivan said, "All right, Sasha, why don't you tell us what you think happened."

So Sasha sat down by his father's bed and told the whole story of his meetings with Ferdy.

When he had finished Ivan said, "Well, that is a wonderful story, Sasha, but I'm a practical man, I need some proof."

Sasha grinned. "No problem, Father. When you are better and the snow begins to melt and spring is coming, we will hold a huge celebration to mark your recovery."

"Splendid," shouted Ivan. "But what will that prove?"

"You'll see, Father, you'll see," replied Sasha, and he would say no more.

All that winter Sasha ate no meat and secretly managed to leave most of his food out for the wolves. Each morning it was gone. By the time spring came that year, Ivan was fully recovered and busy working round the village.

Sasha was sweeping the snow off the steps of the house one day when he noticed some green leaves peeping through the snow. "Spring is nearly here," he cried. "We must arrange our celebration very soon."

That night he slipped out and put some food and a new pair of shiny black boots outside the back door. "Ferdy will like these," he thought to himself. "That old pair of mine must be full of holes by now."

CHAPTER 7

As the day of the celebration drew nearer the village was filled with activity. From every house came delicious smells of pies and cakes and dumplings; the porches of the houses were decorated and huge tables with bright tablecloths were set up. Everyone seemed to be busy doing something. Sasha was busy building a platform for the band to play on and Olga was covering it with a beautiful embroidered cloth. Ivan wandered up with his accordion.

"I never saw such preparations," he commented.

"Well, this is a double celebration," cried Olga. "Your rescue and the end of winter."

"And you changing your mind about wolves," called Sasha, his mouth full of nails.

"I haven't changed my mind yet," laughed his father. "You still haven't given me that proof you promised."

"I will, Father. Never fear, I will."

That night the villagers ate and drank and laughed and sang and danced as they never had before. Sasha danced till his feet hurt but kept his eyes on the spot on the hill where Ferdy used to dance.

At about midnight Sasha picked up a flare, ran over to Ivan and grabbed him by the arm. "Come on, Father, bring your accordion and keep on playing."

"Where are we going, Sasha?"

"To give you your proof."

They climbed up the hill, and while Ivan stood playing, Sasha held up the flare to reveal Ferdy leaping and twirling in his shiny new boots.

"Hello, Sasha man-child. Look at me in my new boots."

"You look great, Ferdy."

"Nothing to do with the boots," grinned Ferdy. "It's just because I'm so good-looking."

Sasha laughed. "Let me introduce my father Ivan, Ferdy," he said.

"We've met," yelled Ferdy, leaping ever higher. "Head feeling better?"

Ivan stopped playing the accordion and stared at Ferdy with his mouth hanging open.

"Music," demanded the wolf. "I can't dance without music."

"Well, er yes," mumbled Ivan, "but please first let me, er, thank you ..."

"No thanks," snapped the wolf, "all I want is music, Sasha man-child's father, music and an end to the wolf hunts."

In a daze Ivan began playing again.

"I can jump higher than you, Sasha man-child," shrieked Ferdy. "Come on, see if you can jump higher than me."

"I will," shouted Sasha, "but only down in the village where it's flat."

"I'm not daft, man-child, I'm not going down there," replied Ferdy rudely. "It might be a trap."

"I wouldn't do that," replied Sasha angrily. "And you know it, Ferdy."

"Yes," agreed Ferdy, "but he might," and he nodded towards Ivan.

"No indeed," cried Ivan, "I am the headman of the village; the whole village is grateful to you for saving me. To me you are a hero, and when the village knows how you helped me you will be a hero to them too."

Ferdy danced round Ivan. "But I thought *you* thought that the only good wolf was a dead wolf."

"I did," cried Ivan, "but you and my crazy son here have made me see I was wrong. Please do me the favour of coming down to the village to be our guest of honour at the celebration for my rescue."

"Ha!" cried Ferdy. "The guest of honour, aye? Me! What a giggle, what a laugh." Ivan roared with laughter, too, and slapped Ferdy on the back.

"So what do you say, Mr Wolf, yes or no?"

"Oh, why not. I believe in living dangerously," said Ferdy. "I will throw caution to the winds." And the three of them walked down to the village, Ivan playing his accordion and Sasha and Ferdy dancing together.

As they entered the village, the villagers fell silent and mothers grabbed

their children and hid.

"Come back, everyone. I, Ivan, your headman and former great wolf-hater, order you back."

Slowly and suspiciously the villagers crept back. There were murmurs of:

"He's mad."

"That blow on the head did it."

"That's right, he's not been himself since."

"Yes, and his son's no better."

Ivan climbed onto the stage. "Friends," he cried. "Good people. I hear you say that I am crazy, that Ivan the wolf-hater has gone mad. No, my friends, not at all, for this wolf here saved my life. He dragged me from the snowdrift and took me to the hut and lit a fire."

"Wolves can't light fires."

"Jolly well can!" interrupted Ferdy. "Better than people, I can tell you!"

"The wolf can talk," cried someone, while the others stared in stunned silence.

"'Course I can talk," grumbled Ferdy.

"What do you think I am, stupid or something? People – honestly!"

Sasha leapt up onto the platform beside his father. "Friends, you have known me all my life. When I was a boy and he was a cub I met this wolf, Ferdy, and we have been friends ever since. Now Ferdy is an excellent dancer and he has challenged me to a leaping

competition. So clear a space and you can be the judge of who dances best and jumps the highest, me or my wolf friend."

Approving murmurs went up from the crowd. Everyone loved a competition.

Sasha jumped down from the stage and pulled up his sleeves. "Are you ready, Ferdy?"

"Certainly am, man-child," came the reply.

Ivan played a chord as a signal for the band to begin. The villagers stood in a circle and clapped while Sasha and Ferdy folded their arms and danced on their heels. Then they began to leap. Sasha leapt high but each time Ferdy leapt higher. Then Sasha began to pant and feel short of breath and hold his side.

"Stop, Ferdy," he cried, "I'm exhausted."

"I'm not," shouted Ferdy. "We wolves are tougher than that. I challenge everyone to a competition."

One after another the youths of the village tried their luck against Ferdy but none of them could compare with the wolf. Gradually the villagers became aware of eyes watching them from the trees behind the schoolhouse.

"It's my pack," yelled Ferdy. "Come on in, I'm showing all the people how to dance. I'm a hero, and I'm a champion. Come on in, wolves, come and watch me show the people how to dance." Slowly the wolves walked into the village, looking around suspiciously, their teeth bared, a snarl on their lips.

Some of the people began to cheer. Sasha walked over to one of the wolves and bowed. "May I have the pleasure of this dance?"

"Go on," said Ferdy. "Give him a thrill, my love. Dance with him. That's my friend Sasha, the man-child, he's all right. That's my wife, Sasha. I taught her how to dance and gave her your old boots."

So Sasha danced with the wolf and Ferdy danced with Olga. Soon everyone was joining in; wolves and people dancing and having fun together.

After a while the music stopped and Ivan cried, "There is lots of food left over. Maybe the wolves are hungry and would like some."

"Oh, we're always hungry," Ferdy agreed cheerfully. "Particularly at the end of winter."

So the villagers put all the spare food on the ground and the wolves ate it all up eagerly.

When it was all gone Ferdy picked up a napkin and wiped his mouth. "Delicious," he said. "I don't know which was best, the cabbage dumplings

or the liver pie?"

"I made the cabbage dumplings!" cried one woman, glowing with pleasure. "I'm so glad you liked them."

"And I made the liver pie," said old Peter. "It's my own recipe."

"Wonderful," sighed Ferdy. "A dream, a dream."

Old Peter grinned from ear to ear with delight. "I could make one for you from time to time," he said.

"And I could leave out some dumplings," called another.

"I often have some fresh bread to spare," said someone else.

"That would be most kind," replied Ferdy. "We wolves really appreciate good cooking, it puts us in a good mood."

Sasha grinned to himself. "That clever old wolf is really making the peace," he thought.

Ivan climbed onto the platform with a silver cup.

"Friends!" he cried. "Both people and wolves. This has been a night for us to remember and celebrate. We've all had fun and, even better, we've all made friends of our former enemies. So I want to make a presentation of the silver cup to Ferdy – the greatest jumper in the area." Everyone cheered.

Ferdy ambled onto the platform and took the cup. "I want to share it with Sasha man-child," he told the crowd. "He's almost as good as me and he's my friend. He gave me my first pair of boots and taught me to dance." Everyone cheered again and Sasha and Ferdy held the cup up together.

"You were right, Sasha," whispered Ferdy, grinning his wicked wolf's grin. "Wolves and people can be friends."

It will not surprise you to learn that after that night the villagers always left food out for the wolves in the hard days of winter. "We may have a little less food," they said, "but at least we don't have to worry about the wolves attacking our animals and our children."

Whenever there was any music or dancing in the village, the sound of fun and laughter echoed throughout the steppe and forest.